Strawberry Shortcake's World of Friends

Grosset & Dunlap

Visit www.strawberryshortcake.com to join the Friendship Club and redeem your Strawberry Shortcake Berry Points for "berry" fun stuff!

GROSSET & DUNLAP
Published by the Penguin Group
Penguin Group (USA) Inc., 375 Hudson Street, New York, New York 10014, U.S.A.
Penguin Group (Canada), 90 Eglinton Avenue East, Suite 700, Toronto, Ontario, Canada M4P 2Y3
(a division of Pearson Penguin Canada Inc.)
Penguin Books Ltd, 80 Strand, London WC2R 0RL, England
Penguin Ireland, 25 St Stephen's Green, Dublin 2, Ireland
(a division of Penguin Books Ltd)
Penguin Group (Australia), 250 Camberwell Road, Camberwell, Victoria 3124, Australia
(a division of Pearson Australia Group Pty Ltd)
Penguin Books India Pvt Ltd, 11 Community Centre, Panchsheel Park, New Delhi - 110 017, India
Penguin Group (NZ), Cnr Airborne and Rosedale Roads, Albany, Auckland 1310, New Zealand
(a division of Pearson New Zealand Ltd)
Penguin Books (South Africa) (Pty) Ltd, 24 Sturdee Avenue, Rosebank, Johannesburg 2196, South Africa

Penguin Books Ltd, Registered Offices:
80 Strand, London WC2R 0RL, England

AMERICAN GREETINGS
American Greetings and rose logo is a trademark of AGC, Inc.

ISBN 0-448-44101-2   10 9 8 7 6 5 4 3 2 1

![Strawberry Shortcake logo]

Strawberry Shortcake's World of Friends

By Megan E. Bryant
Illustrated by Lisa Workman

Grosset & Dunlap

Get Ready...
Get Set...

I'm berry excited! Tomorrow I'm setting off for a trip around the world to visit some berry special friends. Crêpes Suzette, Tea Blossom, Tangerina Torta, and Frosty Puff are great pen pals—and I can't wait to see them all again!

THINGS TO PACK

T-shirts

Sweaters

Shorts

Jeans

Skirts

Dresses

Pajamas

Toothbrush

Shoes

And I can't forget my special scrapbook. I'm going to write down everything I do on my trip!

Pupcake wants to come with me!

Since I'm going to be gone for a while, Apple Dumplin', Custard, and Pupcake will have to stay at home. Angel Cake is going to take care of them. I know she will do a berry good job!

And Away We Go!

First thing in the morning, it's time to take off in my strawberry hot-air balloon. I love flying in the sky with all the clouds!

Good-bye, friends!
I promise I'll be back berry soon!

From the desk of
Strawberry Shortcake

PLACES AND FRIENDS TO VISIT:

Crêpes Suzette in Pearis

Frosty Puff in Niceland

Tea Blossom in
Plum Blossom Province

Tangerina Torta in
Tangerine Bosque

This map shows the route I'm taking.

And I have a compass to keep me on track—even when my strawberry balloon is high in the sky!

Welcome to Pearis

First stop, Pearis! My friend Crêpes Suzette lives here. Pearis is a berry big city, with lots of twisty little streets. Luckily I have a map, so I won't get lost!

PIEFFEL TOWER

RUE DE LA RUE

I bought some postcards of famous Pearisian landmarks!

ARC DE TRIFLE

Here are some new French words I learned in Pearis.

FRENCH WORDS

friend	amie
strawberry	fraise
pink	rose
happy	heureux
dog	chien
cat	chat
hello	bonjour
good-bye	au revoir

Crêpes are a berry yummy food—they are like thin pancakes! You can eat crêpes for any meal—breakfast, lunch, dinner, or dessert. My favorite crêpes have strawberries in them, *mais oui*. (That means "but of course"!)

Crêpes

Make sure an adult helps you make these crêpes!

INGREDIENTS

1 cup milk
1 cup flour
2 eggs

1 tsp vanilla (for dessert crêpes only)
1 tbsp sugar (for dessert crêpes only)
1 tbsp melted butter

DIRECTIONS

Makes 10 crêpes

1. Mix the milk, flour, and eggs (and sugar and vanilla if you're making dessert crêpes) with a wire whisk or electric mixer. You can also use a blender.
2. Add the butter and continue mixing until the batter is thin and smooth.
3. Heat a frying pan until droplets of water "dance" on it.
4. Pour ¼ cup batter into the pan. When the crêpe bubbles and the edges look dry, flip it. Cook for another few minutes until the other side is done.
5. Fill with your favorite toppings! Vegetables and cheese make a nice crêpe for lunch or dinner. Fruit, whipped cream, or chocolate are all yummy fillings for a dessert crêpe!

Meet Crêpes Suzette

Here's a picture of my berry good friend Crêpes Suzette. Crêpes is berry, berry fashionable. She's one of Pearis's best designers! She even has her own design shop and boutique. It's called Chez Crêpes. Crêpes can always tell what's going to be fashionable before it's in style, and she always knows just what to add to make an outfit look berry nice—I mean, *très bien!*

Crêpes's favorite word is "voilà"! (That means "there it is"!)

Crêpes has a pet poodle named Éclair. Éclair is just as stylish as Crêpes Suzette. Every week she goes to a puppy beauty parlor. Ooh la la!

Some of Crêpes's
favorite things are:

FASHION MAGAZINES

RIBBONS

CROISSANTS

GOING ON PICNICS

BERETS

BIKE RIDING
(IN PEARIS A BIKE IS CALLED A VÉLO)

Here's
a picture of
Chez Crêpes.
I can't wait
to go inside
and try on
some of the
berry pretty
fashions!

Ooh la la!

Crêpes had a berry special surprise for me at her boutique—she helped me design and make my berry own outfit! Here's how we did it.

This is a page from Crêpes Suzette's sketchbook. Whenever she has an idea for a new outfit, she draws a picture of it. Crêpes says that's what all the berry best designers do.

Crêpes helped me design an outfit, too. I wanted a dress with a little coat—it gets chilly at the top of the Pieffel Tower!

Then Crêpes helped me pick out just the right kind of material for my dress and coat. She gave me little pieces of cloth so I could see and feel all the fabrics. I like the pink one best!

Crêpes showed me how to sew my new outfit together, too.

These are some of her sewing supplies:

NEEDLE   THREAD   THIMBLE   TAPE MEASURE   PINS   SCISSORS   PATTERN PIECES

And the finishing touch for my new dress and hat? *Voilà*—a strawberry vine!

The berry best trim!

Très chic!
(That means "berry fashionable"!)

I was sad to say good-bye to Crêpes Suzette, but she promised she would come visit me soon in Strawberryland. I can't wait!

Next Stop, Niceland!

I'm berry excited to see my friend Frosty Puff. She lives far away in Niceland, a place that's berry chilly but full of the nicest friends you'll ever meet! Before we land, I have to bundle up with a warm sweater, mittens, a scarf, and a hat. *Brrr!* It's cold outside!

COZY MITTENS

SNUGGLY SWEATER

CUDDLY SCARF

WARM HAT

And I can't forget the things I'll need to play outside in the snow!

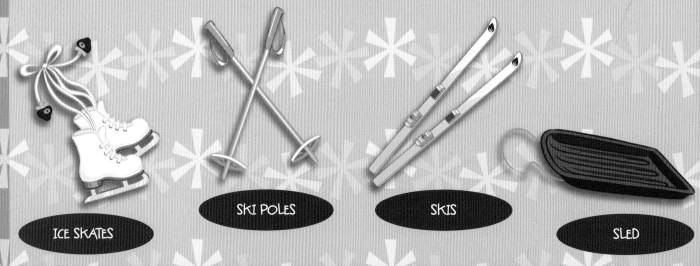

ICE SKATES

SKI POLES

SKIS

SLED

ICELANDIC WORDS

book	bók
fun	gaman
friend	vinur
hello	halló
good-bye	bless
yummy	ljúffengur
cozy	notalegur
snow	snjór

Frosty Puff promised to take me on a tour of Niceland. We're going to see volcanoes, geysers, and the famous Northern Lights.

I was berry surprised when a real volcano erupted!
Red-hot bubbling cherry jam flowed down the side of it.
Frosty told me that when the jam cools it becomes sticky and thick. Wow!

Meet Frosty Puff

Frosty Puff is a berry special friend. Her house is made out of a two-scoop ice-cream cone! Even though it's chilly in Niceland, Frosty Puff's house is cozy and warm inside. I think it's because Frosty has such a friendly heart. You feel happy just being around her!

This is Freezer Pop, Frosty's pet penguin. He's berry cute! Frosty made him this scarf and he wears it every day.

Frosty Puff loves:

EARMUFFS

SNOW CONES

READING BOOKS

COCOA WITH MARSHMALLOWS

ICE-SKATING

WRITING STORIES

# Cozy Cocoa

Ask an adult to help you make this cocoa!

INGREDIENTS

2 cups milk

4 tbsp cocoa powder

 ½ cup sugar

DIRECTIONS   Serves 2

1. Mix together the cocoa powder and the sugar in a small bowl.

2. In a small pot over low heat, warm the milk.

3. Add the cocoa and sugar mixture one tablespoon at a time, stirring until the cocoa has just the right amount of chocolate for you!

4. You can add marshmallows or whipped cream and chocolate shavings for an extra-special treat.

Frosty Puff always has an extra mug of hot cocoa or a snuggly blanket to share if you're feeling cold or lonely. Frosty makes the best hot chocolate ever! I liked it so much, she gave me the recipe.

Winter Wonderland

There are so many fun things to do in Niceland! Frosty Puff and I love sledding and skating.

We skated on flavored ice ponds . . . and sledded down the Ice Cream Hills.

Lots of Snow Fun!

Here is a picture of me in front of the Northern Lights. They look just like sparkly waves of spun sugar twisting and turning in the sky, making everything shimmer and glimmer!

Winter nights can be berry long and quiet in Niceland. Frosty Puff likes to pass the time by writing stories! She's one of the berry best storytellers I've ever met. Here is a story we wrote together:

The Little Star

Once upon a time, there was a twinkly little star that lived up, up, up in the sky, high above the whole wide world. When the sun came up, the little star slept, and when the moon came out, the little star shone brightly, because that's what stars do. Sometimes the little star felt lonely, high up in the sky all by herself. Then the moon told the little star that all around the world, people were looking up at her and thinking happily of their faraway friends. That made the little star happy, too, and from then on she shined her brightest and twinkled all night long.

The End.

I've had a berry nice time visiting Frosty Puff! I hope she comes to see me in Strawberryland soon. I already miss her!

Pack Up for Plum Blossom Province!

One of my berry favorite people in the whole wide world lives berry far away, in Plum Blossom Province. Tea Blossom was born in the land of spiced tea and the Great Wall of Chocolate. I wish my friend Huckleberry Pie could see the Great Wall of Chocolate with me! Huck just *loves* chocolate!

CHINESE WORDS

friend	péngyou
tea	cháyè
flower	huā
panda	xióngmāo
kite	fengzheng
noodles	miàntiáo
hello	ní hao
good-bye	zàijiàn

The Great Wall of Chocolate stretches all the way across Plum Blossom Province. It's amazing!

I learned these Chinese words when I visited Plum Blossom Province.

Meet Tea Blossom

Tea Blossom owns a little tea shop full of all kinds of old-fashioned things—and hundreds of kinds of tea, of course! Tea Blossom is nice as can be and she knows everything about tea, flowers, and being a good friend. Best of all, she is a berry good listener. I'm so glad I know her!

Tea Blossom's special pet is Marza Panda. He keeps her company wherever she goes!

Some of Tea Blossom's favorite things are:

-O-N-G NOODLES   ALMOND COOKIES   TEA (OF COURSE!)   KITES   LANTERNS

Let's Go Fly a Kite

Tea Blossom and I made our berry own kites! We made the kite frames out of special wood called bamboo. (Bamboo is Marza Panda's favorite food, so we gave him a piece to chew on!) Then we covered the frames with pretty silk and made long, flowy tails.

Finally, we painted designs on the kites. They looked berry beautiful!

We spent the whole afternoon flying the kites we made. Afterward we were berry hungry. So Tea Blossom made her favorite treat—almond cookies. They were delicious!

Almond Cookies

Always make these sweet cookies with an adult!

INGREDIENTS

2 sticks butter, softened
1 cup sugar
2 eggs
1½ tbsp almond extract

2½ cups flour
⅛ tsp salt
½ tsp baking soda
whole or sliced almonds

DIRECTIONS   *Makes 24 cookies*

1. Preheat the oven to 425°. Cream the butter and sugar with a mixer. Then mix in the eggs and almond extract.
2. In a separate bowl, combine the flour, salt, and baking soda. Then add the flour mixture to the butter mixture and mix until dough is crumbly.
3. Roll the dough so that it is ½ inch thick. Use cookie cutters to cut lots of shapes! Put an almond in the middle of each cookie.
4. Bake on a foil-covered tray for 12 to 15 minutes.

Berry Beautiful Blooms!

Behind Tea Blossom's tea shop, there is a berry wonderful flower garden! Some of the flowers were the same kind that Orange Blossom grows—but other flowers I had never seen before. Tea Blossom let me pick and press one of each kind for my scrapbook!

AZALEA

WINTERSWEET

CHRYSANTHEMUM

ORCHID

LILY

PEONY

NARCISSUS

LOTUS

PLUM BLOSSOM

ROSE

CAMELLIA

How to Press Flowers

1. Pick flowers to press. Make sure they are dry.

2. Arrange the flowers on a piece of waxed paper. Make sure they are not overlapping or touching.

3. Place another piece of paper over the flowers.

4. Carefully put the flowers in the middle of a thick book, then gently close the book. You can put another large book on top.

5. Wait 3 to 7 days, then check your flowers. If they are all flat, dried out, and papery, they are ready! You can use your dried flowers in an art project or share them with a friend.

Tea for Two

One of the berry nicest things I did in Plum Blossom Province was drink tea in a special Tea Ceremony. At first I thought a Tea Ceremony would be just like a tea party back in Strawberryland—but it's actually berry different!

First, Tea Blossom swished hot water around in a small clay teapot. She used a tiny scoop to put loose tea in the pot and added more hot water. Tea Blossom filled the tea cups only halfway because the other half is supposed to be full of good thoughts for friends. That's the nicest thing I've ever heard!

Before you drink the tea, you are supposed to smell it. I thought it smelled sweet and fresh, like grass or a garden. The first time I tried the tea, I didn't like the taste berry much. Tea Blossom repeated the tea ceremony with lots of different kinds of tea. The more I tried the tea, the more I started to like it!

Saying good-bye to Tea Blossom wasn't easy—but I know I'll see her again soon.

To Tangerine Bosque!

My trip around the world is almost over—but it wouldn't be complete without a visit to Tangerine Bosque! My friend Tangerina Torta lives there, and I can't wait to see her again.

Tangerine Bosque is a little clearing in the middle of a great big rain forest. There's a bright blue lake surrounded by all kinds of fruit trees.

There are lots and lots of amazing natural places in and around Tangerine Bosque. I brought my hiking boots and thick socks because I want to visit them all!

These monkeys live in the rain forest. They play the drums berry well!

Tangerina lives in a cabin way up high in one of the trees! You have to climb a rope ladder to get up to her house.

Here are some new Portuguese words I learned in Tangerine Bosque.

PORTUGUESE WORDS

friend	amiga
hello	olá
good-bye	adeus
nature	natureza
map	mapa
tree	árvore
flower	flor
animal	animal

Meet Tangerina Torta

Tangerina Torta knows just about everything about nature! She loves living deep in the forest. Almost every day, Tangerina takes people on safari tours. She shows them all kinds of exotic plants and wild animals, and teaches them how to take care of the whole world around them. What a berry important job! I'm really looking forward to going on a nature hike with Tangerina. Who knows what we'll see in the jungle?

Banana Bongo is such a funny little monkey! He lives with Tangerina and is her berry best friend.

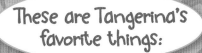
These are Tangerina's favorite things:

CANTEEN

HIKING STICK

COMPASS

TROPICAL FRUIT

BEADED BRACELETS

One of the berry best things that happened in Tangerine Bosque was seeing a triple rainbow! I didn't know there could be more than one rainbow in the sky at a time. Wow!

RULES OF THE RAIN FOREST

⏱ Leave the jungle exactly the way you found it! Don't take rocks, sticks, or plants. (You can take lots of pictures, though!)

⏱ Don't feed the animals—they know how to find just the food they need.

⏱ Make sure you take your trash with you—don't leave it behind.

⏱ Bring water, a map, and a first-aid kit with you—just in case.

⏱ And don't go on a nature walk without telling a grown-up where you're going—or better yet, take one with you!

Before we went on our nature walk, Tangerina taught me some important rules. I wrote them down so I would never forget them!

This is a map of the trail we took through the rain forest.

Here are some animals we saw on our nature walk:

CENTIPEDES AND MILLIPEDES—EEEK!

GIANT FLUTTERY BUTTERFLIES

MARMOSET

LOTS OF BATS!

MONKEYS

After a long day of hiking and exploring, Tangerina Torta and I were berry thirsty! She made a yummy tropical fruit punch. I will definitely make it on hot summer days in Strawberryland!

Tropical Fruit Punch

Have an adult help you make this yummy fruit punch.

INGREDIENTS

- 4 cups pineapple juice
- 2 cups orange or tangerine juice
- 1 cup cranberry juice
- 2 tangerines, split into sections

DIRECTIONS   Serves 4

1. Combine the different juices in a large punch bowl and serve. Make sure they are chilled.

2. Add tangerine slices right before serving for a sweet burst of citrus!

I had a berry wild time visiting Tangerina Torta! I'm so glad she's my friend. I hope we see each other again soon!

It's time to go home now—my trip around the world is over. I had a berry great time! But I'm starting to feel a little homesick for Strawberryland. I miss Apple Dumplin', Custard, Pupcake, and all my friends back home. I can't wait to see them all!

Home Sweet Home

Hooray! I'm back home at last! I think everybody in Strawberryland missed me just as much as I missed them. My friends wanted to hear all about my trip!

Angel Cake tries on my pretty dress!

Ginger Snap flies the kite I made with Tea Blossom.

Orange Blossom wants to go to Tangerine Bosque someday.

Huck tries some chocolate from the Great Wall of Chocolate!

Blueberry Muffin reads the story I wrote with Frosty Puff.

Apple Dumplin' just wants to snuggle.

Good Night, Little Star

It takes a while to get everything unpacked and put away. By the time I'm done, it's bedtime! I'm berry tired from my trip . . . and berry happy to be home . . . and I miss my friends berry much. But when I look out the window, I see one bright star shining down. It makes me think of the story I wrote with Frosty Puff! And I know that everywhere, all over the world, my friends are looking at the same little star.

Tangerina Torta

Marza Panda

Crêpes Suzette

Éclair
©TCFC

Tea Blossom

Frosty Puff
©TCFC

Banana Bongo
©TCFC

©TCFC

©TCFC

©TCFC

On the Go Girl

©TCFC

©TCFC

Freezer Pop
©TCFC

©TCFC

©TCFC

©TCFC

©TCFC

©TCFC

©TCFC

©TCFC

©TCFC

Au revoir!
©TCFC

©TCFC

©TCFC

©TCFC

©TCFC